CALENDRICAL REGRESSION

A NOVELLA OF THE AMAZING CONROY

LAWRENCE M. SCHOEN

COPYRIGHT

Calendrical Regression © 2014 Lawrence M. Schoen.

This book is a work of fiction. All the characters and events portrayed in this book are fictitious. Any resemblance to real people or events is purely coincidental.

Proofreading done by Barbara E. Hill, Kathryn Sullivan, J. V. Ackermann, and Diane Osborne

© 2019 Paper Golem.

Cover art by Tulio Brito.
Book design by Lawrence M. Schoen.
Author photo by Nathan Lilly.

Trade paperback ISBN: 978-1-7326343-8-1
Ebook ISBN: 978-1-7326343-7-4

Vers. 21010

For Jay Lake,
a fellow traveler in time

ACKNOWLEDGMENTS

I put the words on the page,
but this story would never have happened
without a lot of help. My thanks to:

Barbara, who reappeared with timely grace,
Fran, who gave me a simile when I needed one,
Valerie, because she's everything.

CALENDRICAL REGRESSION

A NOVELLA OF THE AMAZING CONROY

THE PIRATE QUEEN was a young brunette who in another life might have been a celebrity spokesperson. She glanced down at her wounded arm, attempted to raise it and failed. Instead she passed her photonic cutlass to her other hand. The move required less than a second, and to the chagrin of her alien opponent she brought the blade up in an effective block and managed to force him back. He stumbled and an instant later she struck the weapon from his grasp in a shower of high velocity sparks that caused his phlox-colored hair to stand on end.

"Where does a pirate learn to do that?" gasped the Auditor in Black, his fishbelly white skin a stark contrast to his ebony suit — marking him as a Clarkeson, a colony creature pretending to be a humanoid. His feet slid on the ever slicker surface of the dirigible as it descended toward the swamp below and the humid air condensed upon its skin.

"I wasn't always a pirate, Hiram," she replied, bringing her cutlass closer and forcing him to his knees. "Before my airship began harrying your tax collectors, I was a princess of the realm, and the darling of Daddy's fencing master."

"What happens now?" asked the Clarkeson, smirking despite

defeat. "Am I your prisoner? You cannot bring me to trial; I'm not accountable to the courts of Earth."

"I've never been a fan of the legal system. Simpler just to kill you."

Hiram laughed. "Gutting me a like human won't end me. I'm not a singular being like you. My sapience results from the collective efforts of more than a million self-aware cellular collectives working in committee."

"Then I'll just have to carve you up into lots of little pieces and scatter them overboard into the swamp. Goodbye, my Lord Auditor. Your committee is hereby disbanded."

She raised the photonic cutlass above her head in preparation for the first stroke.

"Wait! Who's that behind you?"

The pirate queen's contempt at the ploy was palpable. "Please. You can't expect that to actually work. We're fighting on top of a sinking airship, and any harness lines someone might use to climb up here are in front of me."

That's when I reached from behind her, lightly grasped the wrist of her upraised hand, and commanded, "Sleep!" Her body went limp. She slumped against me as her head lolled upon her chest. I caught her as she collapsed and half-dragged / half-carried her a short distance to deposit her in a folding chair at the center of the stage.

The Auditor in Black wasn't a Clarkeson at all but actually a blue-collar worker from Des Moines named Hiram Gustuvson. He'd also succumbed to my command and lay sprawled, illuminated by a spotlight on the stage that mere moments ago had seemed to be the slippery surface of a dirigible. He was bigger than the recent pirate queen and I didn't want to drag him. A quick whisper in his ear, and he stood up, eyes blinking. I guided him back to the chair next to his foe. Next, I stepped behind her chair and brought my lips close to her ear, speaking softly to her as I brought her back to full wakefulness. Then I turned to the audience.

"Ladies and gentlemen, it has been your great fortune to witness, for the first time anywhere, this performance of the *Revenge of the Pirate Queen!* Please show your appreciation for our players, who, despite having no history of pointless violence or weapons training, nonetheless slaughtered dozens of imaginary foes before finally confronting one another for your entertainment."

Thunderous applause met my dazed volunteers. They grinned sheepishly, looked to one another, and—better than I could have choreographed it—joined hands, rose to their feet, and took a bow. It was a great end to the last of a week of shows. Seven days I'd taken off from my regular, unwelcome job as CEO of a hugely successful corporation, a vacation spent returning to my original profession as a stage hypnotist. I'm the Amazing Conroy, and I'm very good at what I do, when I can get away to do it.

The applause ended and I escorted my recent hypnotic subjects off the stage and into the waiting arms of their friends and colleagues. One of the small tables in front stood vacant now. Earlier, I'd invited its occupant on stage as a volunteer but she'd demurred. At some point in the show she'd slipped away, her escape covered by darkness, obscured by spotlights, and masked by the antics on stage.

I bid everyone a good night and, as soon as the stage lights went dark, I slipped through the rear curtain, ending my week of headlining at the Hotel Rotundo in downtown Omaha.

I'd been putting in two shows a night to an audience that had consisted of the attendees of several different groups that had opted to hold their national meetings there in Nebraska, including the Association of Midwestern Pipefitters, Mothers Against Migraines, and my personal favorite the Royal Order of Otters. It wasn't a bad gig as far as such things went; Omaha rarely attracts really big name acts, so a stage hypnotist can do pretty well. But I wasn't there for the money. A couple years earlier I'd stumbled into a venture breeding and leasing buffalo dogs and I was now richer than I had any right to be. The work had taken me to Mars a month earlier, and after returning to Earth, I'd decided to treat myself to a little time off. When I had mentioned this to my secretary, she promptly presented me with an array of terrestrial vacation spots featuring a nice assortment of white sandy beaches, private forests, and mountain vistas. Moreover, each included nearby, five-star restaurants that catered to ultra-rich humans and a wide range of xenophilic aliens.

I was tempted. The venues were all variations on paradise, obscenely expensive, and well within my budget. But it was neither what I wanted nor needed. I had no use for paradise, though I almost relented after reviewing the restaurants' menus. In the end, my resolution held and I slipped away by returning to my earlier career, leaving the running of my company in the hands of people who knew what they were doing far better than me. Instead, to the horror of my security chief, I called in a favor from a friend in the stage performers' union and within an hour had gotten myself booked at the Hotel Rotundo to perform my hypnosis act and make utter strangers believe outlandish suggestions for the entertainment of others.

It had been a glorious and restful week, but as I undid the knot of my bowtie and walked down the backstage corridor to my dressing room, I knew it was time to hang up my tuxedo and return to the corporate office back in Philadelphia.

The woman waiting for me in the hallway changed all that.

She was the same woman who'd vanished before the end of my show, vacating a front table that usually went to master plumbers or reverend otters of great distinction. In hindsight, I should have taken that as an omen.

When selecting volunteers for a show I tend toward two types: either the sort of ordinary person who blends in and goes through life otherwise unnoticed, and at the other extreme someone who has made a significant, though not necessarily conscious, effort to stand out. This woman fell into the second group.

A single glance revealed that she wasn't from the Midwest. Her tanned skin had that perfect seamless look that only comes from salons in New York or L.A., where you spend ten minutes hanging in zero gee while melanin wielding nano-machines paint your epidermis one cell at a time. I assumed a similar treatment had been applied to her shoulder length blonde hair; it had an otherworldly look, the way it bounced in curly streamers all around her head. She probably came by her dimples honestly and they worked to give her a girl-next-door flavor that was at odds with the perfection of skin and hair. Her clothes didn't help things. Sure, we were in Omaha, but the rest of my audience still made a point of showing up in the latest definition of 'office casual.' The men all had collared shirts and the women all wore dresses. She had clothed herself in new jeans and an oversized sports jersey representing a team from the Martian dustball minor league. I'd followed the disapproving glances of more than one of the women gathered in Omaha to rally against migraines when I'd sought her out as a volunteer. When she turned down my invitation, I'd switched to a pretty plumber and put her out of my mind.

Now she stepped back into it, having apparently left my show early the better to lay in wait for me in the dilapidated hallway backstage. She stood there now, leaning against the door to my dressing room, the shiny blue fabric of her Helium Hurlers jersey stretched in interesting ways across her torso. I stopped a few feet away, still trying to determine if she was a groupie or a crazie. Neither were unheard of in my field, though the latter were more common.

If she was a crazie, I certainly didn't want her coming into my dressing room. For that matter, while it would be flattering if she were a groupie, I wasn't looking for that sort of thing either. It was Friday night and I had a ticket for a redeye back home with a plan to spend the weekend catching up on my sleep and dining at a couple of five-star restaurants. All too quickly it'd be Monday morning, and I'd be expected to show up at the corporate offices of Buffalogic, Inc. bright and early to resume reviewing business proposals and taking meetings with corporate leaders from all over the Earth and beyond. So, regardless of her story, or my own wishful thinking, she wasn't going to be joining me in my dressing room.

"Good evening, Mr. Conroy. My name is Nicole. I very much enjoyed your show tonight. The things you made your volunteers do, I've never seen anything like it."

I offered up a tight smile, nodding my head to acknowledge the praise, and had pretty much decided she belonged in the groupie category. "Thank you, you're very kind. But, if you'll excuse me, I—"

"And that last part where you made that plumber believe he was a Clarkeson? Incredible. It was spot on. Plots within plots with them. Have you met many Clarkesons?"

An odd question, but then I'd already pegged her as a bit more worldly than the rest of the audience. "A few," I answered. "Thanks for coming. I'm glad you enjoyed the show. Now I really must—"

"You know, my uncle saw one of your earliest performances, what was it, fourteen years ago? On Hesnarj."

It was like she'd slapped me. Hesnarj was an alien mausoleum world where I'd been marooned while a college student. There'd been precious few humans anywhere on that planet. I'd discovered my talent as a stage hypnotist there, befriended my first aliens, and even met one who had helped me to channel my deceased great aunt Fiona.

I started to reply but she cut me off again.

"But that's not why I'm here. The show was just a delightful bonus. I actually came to meet you for a completely unrelated reason."

Okay, maybe *not* a groupie. "Oh? You did? I see. Well, and that's—"

"There's someone quite extraordinary that I'd like you to meet. His name is Juan Sho. He's involved with sorghum, that and cookbooks."

Sorghum cookbooks? I made a point of looking up and down the length of our empty hallway. Just that quickly the scales had tipped toward crazie.

"He's not here, Mr. Conroy. He's waiting for us in Mexico."

"Mexico?"

She smiled, revealing perfect, gleaming teeth. "Well, yes. Like yourself, he's a busy executive by day, and also shares your passion for cuisine, though in his case it's more about how it's crafted than how it tastes. Right now he's probably in a little restaurant in

Veracruz, reverse-engineering the best mole poblano you've ever had."

This time my smile was genuine. If you can appreciate a truly fine mole then you'll understand why. Excellent food is my weakness and Nicole — whoever she was — had done her homework. Some part of my brain threw away both of the likely pigeonholes I'd laid out for her and tabled further attempts at classification. She had my attention. I unlocked my dressing room and opened the door.

"Really? You know, I've never been to Veracruz. Why don't you come in and tell me more about this."

I don't like being separated from my buffalo dog, but I'd long since learned that bringing him on stage leads to more problems than it solves. Buffalitos can consume *anything*, and the last time I'd let him sit quietly on stage he'd begun chewing through the footlights while I'd been distracted performing a hypnotic induction. Out of necessity, I'd been leaving Reggie behind in the spacious closet that the management at the Hotel Rotundo assured me was their best dressing room. It had just enough space for two chairs and a tiny makeup table positioned in front of a mirror bolted to the wall. Every night before going on stage, I'd been bribing Reggie with a big bowl of ball bearings and peanut butter, extra chunky. It'd done the trick, and when I returned after each show I'd find the bowl empty and my buffalo dog asleep under the table.

Out of necessity, the dressing room's door opened into the hall. I led the way so as not to alarm Reggie. Nicole followed, closing the door behind her. My buffalito had been napping as expected and roused himself with a wide yawn at our arrival. His nose crinkled. His eyes opened wide and locked onto Nicole. With a yip he burst into motion, tiny hooves scraping for purchase against floor tile that had been new back when humanity first set foot on the moon. Reggie hurtled across the scant two meters that separated the back of the room from the door, darting a few steps to the side to put himself in a direct line with Nicole. He launched himself into the air like furry cannonball, aiming to strike her amidships and sink her with a single shot. Whether by simple reflex, dumb luck, or prescience, Nicole brought her arms up and caught him with both hands. She staggered backwards against the door in surprise. The entire sequence took no more than a second or two, during which all I managed to do was turn in place to face them both.

I started to apologize for my buffalito's uncommon behavior but stopped short. Nicole beamed with delight while Reggie licked her face with unabashed joy. Okay, no harm done, but introductions were still in order.

"So... that's Reggie. He's normally very friendly, but I've never seen him take to someone quite so quickly."

"I think it's my perfume," said Nicole, grinning as she struggled to reposition her grip on him. Reggie continued to writhe for a better vantage point, determined to slather as much of her skin as possible. Buffalo dogs are deceptively dense, and while Reggie was small enough that I could comfortably carry him under one arm, Nicole was just over a meter and a half tall and looked to have the muscle of an anemic twelve year old.

"Perfume?" I hadn't noticed any unusual scents, not back in the lounge nor in the closer confines backstage. I inhaled deeply but still nothing.

"It's not important. This just confirms my research, that you're the person my uncle and I thought you were and that we've found you at last."

Years on stage kept the frown from reaching my face, but her remark set off several alarms. Back when I'd been just a hypnotist, I'd discovered how much less than fun actually having a stalker could be. As a hyper-wealthy corporate CEO I had a security specialist whose job included keeping those kind of crazies away from me, and if one had found me when I'd gone off on a private vacation against his advice I'd never hear the end of it — not to mention whatever nonsense this new would-be stalker woman intended as the rightful conclusion of her quest to 'find' me. And what was this about an uncle?

"Yeah, about that—"

Someone in the hallway wrenched the door open, cutting off my train of thought as Nicole stumbled backwards.

The newcomer prevented her from falling, supporting Nicole with its own body, a maneuver that demonstrated either practice or long planning. Its dark clothing — a hooded poncho and baggy slacks — hid its identity, revealing only a glimpse of rough grey skin at hand and cheek. One arm came around to encircle Nicole's torso, pinning her right arm to her side, while its other arm moved underneath her left, that hand coming to rest against her clavicle, where it held a shiny, faceted device firmly against Nicole's throat.

In that instant, I recognized not only the race of the alien that had just invaded my dressing room, but also the weapon. The first part was easy. Only the Svenkali had skin that looked like a layer of tiny, grey pebbles. As for the device, I'd only seen one once, fifteen years before, when a different Svenkali had pressed it against my own throat. It was called a *peeler*, and I'd been scant seconds away from being killed over a misunderstanding of religious proportions. In anyone else's hands the device was nothing more than a pretty paperweight of palladium and crystal, too light to be lethal even as a bludgeon. But I'd since learned that a Svenkali could channel a portion of lifeforce into it, empowering the device to subatomically peel away the layers of its victim's nervous system and leave a clear signature of who had done it.

Whether or not Nicole recognized it or just understood it as a weapon at her throat, she froze in place. She continued to hold my buffalito awkwardly in her outstretched arms. Reggie meanwhile began growling.

I froze too. They were only steps away from me but if the alien wanted her dead, he could activate the peeler and kill her before I could cover half the distance.

He spoke, and at his words Nicole blanched. He used Traveler, a galactic pidgin commonly spoken among aliens of different races, and not something I'd expected a young woman in Nebraska to have understood.

"I am Lorsca, third seeker on the path. You have hidden among others, but you cannot disguise your true self from my mission. You are the Uary. Eight hundred and fourteen Uary have I corrected. Today that number grows. I identify you as your kind have named yourself since the moment of your first, unforgivable offense. Acknowledge this truth as your last fact and I will end you more swiftly than you deserve."

The crystal facets of the Svenkali's peeler gave off a lambent cerulean pulse. Nicole whimpered. Her lips parted as if to respond to his command, but before she could say a word Reggie acted. He writhed in her grasp, craning his face toward the fascinating object in the Svenkali's hand. His muzzle pressed and braced against Nicole's neck. He opened his mouth and his lips engulfed the device from its tip to the edge above where Lorsca gripped it. Reggie bit through the peeler like it was a piece of meringue, chewed twice, and swallowed.

Tiny blue fireworks erupted from the gleaming end of what remained of the weapon. Lorsca cried out, hand spasming backward. The Svenkali stared at the fragment of weapon, a mingled expression of horror and disbelief shone on its pebbly face. Squirming in Nicole's hands, Reggie switched from growling to barking.

The Svenkali reached for Reggie, letting the ruined device slip from its hand as it grabbed him by the back of the neck and yanked him from Nicole's grasp. Reggie yelped and the Svenkali pushed Nicole at me. I caught her, the force of the shove throwing us the remaining distance to the back wall. We crashed into the makeup table as the Svenkali backed out of my dressing room while angrily shaking my buffalo dog.

"This is only a temporary respite," said Lorsca. "Nothing will remove you from my path. I will fashion another instrument for your correction. You will not leave this world."

He slammed the door and an instant later its edges buzzed and merged with the walls and floor. It was as if someone had painted the image of a door on the wall; the actual exit had ceased to exist.

Nicole slumped against me. I cradled her in my arms a moment, then eased her into one of the chairs. I started to reach for the comm on the wall but her hand stopped me.

"What are you doing?"

"Calling hotel security."

"Don't. He's not a danger to anyone but me. They'll only get hurt if they try to stop him."

"He took Reggie!"

She shook her head. "As a point of honor. To ensure that the creature that disrupted his attempt will be present when he completes what he started. Reggie is in no danger."

"Why is a Svenkali hunting you? With a peeler, no less."

"Oh? You recognized the weapon?" She smiled. "Ah, further verification, not that it was needed."

In the aftermath of the moment, pieces began falling into place. The first and last place where I'd met two of the Svenkali, where one had threatened me with a peeler, had been the mausoleum world of Hesnarj, where Nicole had said her uncle had seen me.

"What are you talking about? What's really going on here?"

"Truly, I did not mean to deceive you, Mr. Conroy. My intention was to reveal myself once we had reached the privacy of this chamber. Events... proceeded rapidly in other directions before I could do so."

"Reveal yourself how?" I asked.

She shrugged, gesturing to herself. Any sign of distress over the attempted murder had vanished. "I am not as I appear to be. Not human. It is why Reggie reacted as he did when I entered the room. Buffalitos have always been able to detect my kind."

"And what kind might that be?"

"I am the Uary," she said.

I frowned. I'd met many of the aliens that regularly traveled in Human Space, and knew the names of most of those that I hadn't come across. I didn't recognize hers.

"And the Uary are..."

She paused. An expression fluttered across her face like she wanted to correct me on something but it passed and she answered me.

"The hereditary enemy of the Svenkali, for more than five billion years."

I crossed to a spot just to the left of what used to be the dressing room's only door and kicked at the wall hard enough to break through the plaster. I winced and hopped backwards, wiggling my toes to check if I'd broken something in my foot. Whatever Lorsca had done to the door had affected the rest of the wall too.

I turned back to Nicole. As much as I wanted her to elaborate on the Svenkali's five billion year vendetta, I wanted to get out of that room more. "Is there a way to undo whatever he did?"

She frowned and her eyes glazed over for a moment. As I watched, I'd have sworn her irises changed color from a robin's egg blue to turquoise, and then back as she blinked and tossed her head like someone who'd briefly fallen asleep.

"There is, but we don't have the necessary equipment to restore the molecular bonds. Nor is just the door barred to us; the effect will have spread to the contiguous walls for a distance of at least twelve meters. You'd need power tools to cut through any of them."

"Sorry, I left them in my other tux."

The look she gave me made it clear that she didn't find me as clever as I liked to think I was.

"It shouldn't matter. Lorsca is a hunter-drone. Physically much stronger and swifter than gendered Svenkali, but also much less sophisticated in its thought processes. It rendered the existing door unusable and likewise has blocked us from creating new ones in the wall."

"And that doesn't matter?"

She stood up, climbed onto her chair and stepped from there to the surface of the makeup table, raising her arms above her head and pressing her hands against a panel of the dressing room's drop ceiling. A hard shove later and she was gesturing to the dark space above.

"We should be able to crawl through here until we're on the other side of the wall and then drop back down into the hall."

I followed her onto the table. It wobbled under our combined weight so I wasted little time and helped her clamber up into the area above the ceiling and onto a support beam. Then I pulled myself up and scrambled after her. Two minutes of crawling later and we stood in the hallway, dusty but not otherwise worse for the trip.

Which isn't to say I wasn't more than a little freaked, but I had enough experience to know I needed to gain a better perspective before putting as much distance as possible between Nicole and myself. More importantly, I had to recover Reggie!

I glanced at Nicole, making a mental note to stop thinking of her as a model-perfect human girl and to start thinking of her as a humanoid female from a race of aliens I'd never heard of before. That'd get easier the more I knew.

"Tell me about this whole 'hereditary enemy' thing," I said.

"Here? Now?"

I shrugged and made no sign of moving anywhere. "This is where we happen to be, and the more I understand about this, the better the odds of coming up with a plan to recover Reggie."

"I'm sorry, Mr. Conroy, but I'd like for us to leave here and reconnoiter with my uncle. I've left him a message about what's happened. He's securing transportation for us right now. We can be in Veracruz by dawn."

"You left a message? How? When?"

"When you asked me to check for a way to undo what the Svenkali did to the wall. It's what the Uary does. Please, I'll explain on the way."

"The way to where?"

Her eyes glazed over again. The poor lighting in the hallway prevented me from seeing if they changed color. She blinked once and said, "The airport. Nikos has called a cab for us. He'll have a plane ready to leave by the time we arrive."

"And Nikos is…"

She shrugged, sending her blonde curls dancing in all directions. "I would have introduced him to you as my uncle, but there's no point to that now. He is also the Uary. That's how important this is, Mr. Conroy. The Uary always works alone. Like the Svenkali, our numbers are very limited, and we cannot normally risk that more than one of us will be found at a time."

"But you're making an exception so that you can introduce me to a Mexican cookbook author? That makes no sense."

She smiled that same perfect smile and held out both hands. "I promise I'll explain it all on the way to the airport."

There was no way I was going to Mexico with an unknown alien for some unexplained purpose. But... all I had right then were questions and maybe she or her 'uncle' could answer them. Maybe I wasn't thinking clearly. A different alien with murder in its eye had just stolen my buffalo dog and imprisoned me in my own dressing room. Yeah, I needed to know what was going on and whether I liked it or not, my best source for finding out seemed determined to jump in a cab.

"I haven't said I'm going to Veracruz."

"Understood, but if you change your mind, won't it be convenient to find ourselves already at the airport?"

One end of our hallway led to the stage I'd so recently quit, the other opened onto the employee parking lot behind the hotel. A cab pulled up as we exited and if the driver found anything unusual about picking up a fare there he gave no sign. I held the door for Nicole and we climbed into the backseat.

"The Airfield, please." An instant later we began moving and she sat back and turned her attention to me.

"To understand any of this, you have to begin with a simple premise: The Svenkali believe themselves to be perfect."

"Excuse me?"

"They make a compelling argument. Our galaxy is over thirteen billion years old, and the Svenkali have existed for most of that span. They are extremely long-lived, and even back at the beginning they were not terribly fertile, but it balanced out. From their earliest recorded history they have had the singular ability to invoke the consciousness of any Svenkali who ever lived, to commune with and access all that had ever been known by any of them."

"I... have some familiarity with that."

"Oh yes, you channeled your dead relative. That's part of why I'm here."

"You know about that? How could you know about that?"

She waved my questions away. "Later. We must stay focused. I was speaking of the Svenkali. They developed as all true sapients do, and successfully passed through that adolescence where, if a species manages not to destroy itself, it flourishes and enjoys a technological and/or spiritual renaissance. They poured out into a mostly empty galaxy, expanding into many clusters of planets and satellites and daring adventures in social engineering. They learned, they fought, they transformed, they reinvented. By the end of their first three billion years, they had explored every possibility they could imagine. They shaped their society to embrace certain beliefs and reject others."

"Three billion...?"

She nodded. "They are by all estimates the longest lived race that remains. Fewer than one in ten thousand survives even a billion years, and they have been here for thirteen times that. But I am getting ahead of myself. After three billion years, other sapients were also exploring the galaxy. The Svenkali retreated from tens of thousands of worlds, preferring isolation to interaction. That preference has never changed. For the past ten billion years they have been self-contained. They have no need of us, no need of anyone but themselves. And because they can invoke any ancestor they choose, they are their own beginning, middle, and end."

"And that makes them perfect?"

Nicole shrugged. "I didn't say they were, I said they believe themselves to be. It's worth noting that they never commune with anyone from the time before they locked in to their current ethos. Having rejected those earlier perspectives, they fear possible contamination from them."

"You're saying they've been static for ten billion years?"

"It's not as dramatic as it seems from your perspective. Keep in mind, their average life span is half a million years."

I sagged against the cab's seat and closed my eyes. "Sorry, I'm having some trouble wrapping my head around these orders of magnitude."

"You're a young race with no perspective on galactic history. It's understandable," said Nicole, and we spent the rest of the ride in silence.

Our cab took us out of Omaha on the old Interstate 29, over the Missouri River and into Iowa, causing me to briefly wonder if crossing the state line complicated any possible crime I'd unknowingly involved myself in. The driver took us through a parking lot and past a low building, pulling to a stop in front of a gate in a chainlink fence that, according to the sign, marked one side of a municipal airport in Council Bluffs. Other than a handful of security lights, everything on both sides of the fence lay in darkness. I could make out the general shape of a couple other buildings, presumably locked up tight. As I exited the cab, lights beyond the fence came on, illuminating a runway. A private plane waited at the near end of it. As I approached the gate, a hatch opened in its side. Brighter light spilled out and a silhouetted figure kicked at something which unfolded into a set of steps to the tarmac. He came down them, his speed part illusion caused by a stoop to his posture that had him leaning forwards like a man sprinting, and part due to a pair of short legs working to produce rapid if tiny steps. Despite the greater distance, he reached his side of the gate first and passed through, stepping into the beams of the cab's headlights and revealing himself to be an old man.

"Welcome, Mr. Conroy, I am Nikos."

"Please. I know that's not your real name, any more than your 'niece' is Nicole. And you know that I know it."

He shrugged. "That's what it says on my passport. Nikos Oriekas, of Shaumburg, Illinois."

He moved with a fluid grace that contradicted his apparent age. If I hadn't known he wasn't human, I'd have pegged him at eighty — possibly ninety if he'd been wealthy and well enough connected to purchase one of the legitimate longevity drugs that existed for those with sufficient privilege.

I can't tell you why, but when I'm meeting new people I always look at their chins first. For a man it manifests in a question of whether he has a beard or not, and if so of what style; how is it trimmed and does the facial hair match what's on top. With women, it's about the shape of the chin, the tautness and perceived elasticity of the skin. Nikos Oriekas had a goatee, neatly trimmed, a mixture of black and grey hair that matched the hair on his head. Most people look at the eyes first, not the chin, but that option didn't exist here. Despite the surrounding darkness, Nikos wore lightly tinted wraparound sunshades. These bore more than a passing resemblance to the x-ray visors my childhood friends in less religious households had bought online after hoarding their allowance for weeks. His clothing was unremarkable, the sort of pico-fiber earth-toned leisure suit and collarless linen shirt that would have let him fit in at any retirement community from Sarasota to Seattle. I could well imagine a community room somewhere in a Chicago suburb, filled with similarly dressed oldsters swapping tall tales of their salad days and stories of talented and precocious grandchildren who never came to visit.

And then I glanced down at his shoes, realized that the heels had been built up to add at least five centimeters to his height, and it hit me. Nicole's oversized jerseys had hidden her figure, and Nikos's eyewear covered a good portion of his face, but the size of their heads and hands, the height and breadth and shapes of their lips and noses, were identical. Take away his lifts and the pair were exactly the same height. It went far beyond family resemblance.

"Does it say that on Nicole's passport, too?" I asked. "Or does she bother with one? Do you share?"

Nicole answered for him. "I told you the Uary works alone. What you think you've deduced isn't the main reason, but it's a contributing factor." She finished paying the driver and he pulled away, taking the light with him.

I nodded. "That's the phrasing you used before. You didn't say you were *an* Uary, or *one of* the Uary. You said you're *the* Uary."

"Yes," said Nicole.

"And so is Nikos?"

"I am, Mr. Conroy."

"You're the same person."

"Not... quite so simple, but in many ways, yes," said Nikos. "Unlike your own race, and the other alien races you've likely encountered, we were not born. The seeds from which all the Uary spring were created billions of years ago. Most lay dormant for hundreds of millennia. I was quickened some eighteen centuries ago, Nicole just over one hundred fifty years past."

"Is that why the Svenkali want to kill you? Some sort of protective jealousy of longevity?"

Nikos cocked his head. "Jealousy, yes. But not because of life span. Even without a violent ending we'd live the merest fraction of what they manage. Rather it is because like the Svenkali, the Uary comprises a vast array of experience. Each of us shares everything that we learn to it. And each can access that array, thus all the information any of us has is there for all."

I nodded. It made sense. The Svenkali who had helped me talk to my dead aunt had been banished by his people; none of them would ever invoke him once he died. It didn't take much imagination to think that such a race wouldn't appreciate competition, regardless of whether or not it impinged on them.

Nikos waved my comprehension away with a sweep of his hand. "You think you understand, Mr. Conroy, but you do not. Humans have a singular view of consciousness, but there are other options. The Svenkali experience consciousness in series. Each living being can invoke any who has come before, benefiting from their lives and wisdom. My people approach it in yet another way. Thirty times each day the Uary all reconnect and share. Our experience is unitary, each individual is simply an outward manifestation of a larger whole. In many ways, the system is quite superior to the Svenkali ability."

"So, they want you dead because they resent you?"

"Remember how I said they believe themselves to be perfect?" Nicole had moved to the other side of the gate and waved impatiently for us to follow. "The Uary threatens that belief just by existing. That, and our need to understand and categorize all things. You might find it simpler to think of us as a race of galactic librarians. What we learn, we share with other races; it defines who we are. The Svenkali, on the other hand, have had billions of years to perfect behaving like spoiled children. Their toys are for them alone."

"Okay, that explains why they want to kill you. But what does any of that have to do with me?" Nicole had reached the hatch; she ignored me and boarded the plane. I turned to Nikos, who shrugged.

"As Nicole said, we will tell you everything. But now that Lorsca knows we are on Earth, time is critical. We need to leave for Veracruz at once." Nikos moved to follow her aboard.

"Hold on! I am *not* going to Mexico!"

He paused and turned back to face me. "Mr. Conroy, I assume you want the opportunity to regain your buffalito, yes?"

"Of course!"

"Then one of two things has to happen. Either you must find Lorsca, or it must find you."

"Can you tell me where it is?"

"We cannot. The Svenkali do not travel amidst other races so we can assume Lorsca had a vessel somewhere nearby. Killing the Uary is not enough. It must flay us, body and mind, and there is only one weapon to accomplish that. It will need to return to its craft and fashion a new peeler."

"That doesn't help me to find Reggie," I said.

"There is no need to find him. Lorsca will bring your buffalito with it when it comes to kill us. To ensure your reunion with your creature you need only wait until the assassin appears."

"You're saying I have to go with you, because the Svenkali will track down you and Nicole and have Reggie with it when it does."

"Precisely. And *we* are going to Veracruz, where Mr. Sho is waiting for us. Now, are you coming?" He turned his back to me and followed Nicole onto the plane.

I didn't have any real choice, not if I wanted to get Reggie back. I ran after the Uary and up the steps.

———————

Except, it wasn't really a plane. Sure, it had wings and a fuselage, and all those other plane-shaped parts that pilots and other air-travel aficionados know the names of, everything you'd expect to find on a plane when viewing it from the outside. Inside though, once I stepped past the entryway — which could be seen by someone outside — it was all plasma-walls and gel-beds and interactive foofaraw that highly advanced aliens used when traveling with speed and comfort. In space.

"Why do you have a space yacht disguised as an airplane?"

Nicole had already settled in the pilot's couch well forward of the entryway and her hands danced across some elaborate holographic control interface, laying in the course or maybe just programming the thing to record her favorite soaps on some local midwestern vid channel.

Nearer the rear of the vessel, Nikos reclined on one of the gel-beds and waved me to another. The faintest of quivers in the bed's surface revealed that we had already taken off.

"The Uary has always found it best to blend in wherever we go. It… simplifies things. Thus, when visiting Earth, we present as human and reconfigure our vessel to a local analogue."

Imagine an overly friendly chaise longue and you'll have a reasonable idea of how it feels to lie on a gel-bed. I may not know much about spacecraft, but the only reason to have acceleration furniture was if you had the capability and intention of engaging in some high-gee maneuvers over and above what could be readily absorbed by the technological wizardry that created a spacecraft's gravity in the first place.

"Just how fast are you planning to fly to Veracruz?" It was a question better asked of Nicole, given that she was piloting, but I was beginning to understand that it didn't matter which of them I spoke to, and Nikos was right there.

"We're not actually flying there, Mr. Conroy. That might draw too much attention and could alert Lorsca to our destination. He is, of a certainty, monitoring local air traffic communications. Instead we will employ a translocational slippage using your world's own magnetic field."

"Trans-what?"

"It's a technology for moving between two points on a planet that share the same longitude. It has only limited application, which is why it went out of vogue millions of years ago."

"Then why are you using it?"

"Two reasons: First, because Omaha and Veracruz share approximately the same longitude. And second, because it is so obscure that a Svenkali hunter-drone would never think to scan for it."

"And you just happened to have this obsolete hardware on your ship?"

"Not at all," said Nicole from the front of the vessel. "We acquired it from a consultant."

"A consultant?"

"This is the first time the Uary has come to your world. We required the assistance of a data-broker to locate both Mr. Sho and you. Since your experience with Kwarum on Hesnarj we have followed your career from a distance. But you are only half of the equation. Finding someone with Mr. Sho's pedigree was much harder. He is the direct, patrilineal descendant of a Mayan priest born four thousand years ago."

"Right. And this data-broker just happened to know where you could find such a person?"

"Yes. And yourself as well. He also provided the translocational slippage unit."

"That's nonsense. Finding me is easy, but how would a human consultant be able to trace someone's lineage back four thousand years to a specific person? To say nothing of having a spare, working model of ancient extra-terrestrial technology?"

Nicole glanced over her shoulder, a disapproving expression on her face. "I didn't say he was human. Yours is not the only race on the planet any more. The data-broker was a Clarkeson."

Nikos had somehow rotated his gel-bed around to face me. "Is something wrong, Mr. Conroy? You are becoming upset."

I ignored him and continued questioning Nicole. "A Clarkeson? Is that why you were asking me if I'd ever met any?"

"Indeed. It seemed quite ironic that you would have included the illusion of one in your show."

"That's not ironic, and it's certainly not coincidental, not with a Clarkeson involved. You said something to the same effect yourself."

Nikos shrugged and picked up the conversation. "We had some concerns, but Mr. Sho checked out exactly as the Clarkeson said. And you were right where he told us you would be. It was a mutually beneficial trade of information."

I sat up quickly, or would have if the gel-bed didn't cling and reduce my effort to slow motion. "What information is he getting out of it?"

"The results of your interaction with Mr. Sho."

"What interaction? You still haven't told me what any of this is about."

"It's really quite simple," said Nikos. "We want you to hypnotically regress Mr. Sho. Take him back four thousand years to his many times great grandfather."

"That's crazy! What's the point of that?"

"We're after two things, actually, but what we're hoping to acquire from Mr. Sho's ancestor is information about the Mayan calendar."

I had to pause and rack my brain for a moment. I knew the ancient Mayans had possessed some elaborate calendrical system, but I couldn't think how it might interest the Uary. When in doubt, ask. "What about it?"

"The Long Count of the Mayan calendar reached the conclusion of its thirteenth baktun on December 21st of 2012. Does that date mean anything to you?"

I nodded, still not able to put the pieces together. "Every kid in school knows that date. It was the day of Galactic Contact, when humans discovered we weren't alone."

"Precisely. And it was predicted centuries in advance by the Mayan calendar."

"So? What does this have to do with getting me to hypnotically regress a cookbook writer back four millennia to his priestly ancestor?"

"We want to ask him how they knew."

I stared at Nikos for a moment as conflicting responses battled for the right to exit my mouth, both about his misunderstanding of hypnotic regression and the absurdity of the question he intended to ask. Instead I turned to Nicole and inquired, "So, in rough terms that a non-engineer might understand, how does this translocational slippage work?"

She tapped the board in front of her and an iris opened in the floor to reveal what I assumed was the hardware in question. It looked like a Klein bottle, one of those topological oddities where the inside and the outside are the same surface. It glowed with a faint amber light and deep in its guts I could see a tiny, red, airplane-shaped light.

"I won't try to explain the physics, but on a planetary surface a relationship exists between two points of common longitude that at a varying range of altitude makes it possible to achieve translocation. Essentially, once we have ascended to an acceptable verticality the device will engage and project a field of overlap. For a moment, everything within that field will simultaneously exist in both places and then slip from one to the other. The device powers down and we descend to our destination. At which point we— Oh!"

That was all the warning I had as the not-an-airplane made use of its acceleration couches. Mine flipped up about a hundred degrees, forcing me back into the cushiony embrace of the gel even as I felt like I was leaning over the floor. The floor of course had moved too. We weren't actually falling, but we'd definitely tumbled.

"What's happening?"

Nicole's hands flew wildly across the ship's controls. Closer by, Nikos had likewise been grabbed and held by his gel-bed, but not before losing his sunglasses to the sudden change in orientation. His eyes were a vivid turquoise and he looked to be in a trance, or more likely having some kind of seizure.

"Nicole, something's wrong with Nikos."

"He's fine. I've made an error in judgement and he is consulting the Uary archive for best-case scenarios."

"What's happened?"

"I cannot know for certain, but my guess would be that we are the victims of our own nature."

The ship tumbled again, hard to port. A surprisingly loud clang reverberated through the hull.

"What does that mean?"

"Lorsca profiled us. He took into account our likely familiarity and preference with utilizing outmoded technology and set up countermeasures."

"Lorsca is here?"

She slapped a spot on her board and the wall nearest me shimmered into a view screen. The Svenkali hovered outside the ship. It wore something that looked like an EVA suit with wings and a pair of jet engines. It held a gleaming white bazooka with both hands, which probably explained the earlier noise. There was a writhing sack affixed to its chest, bound in place by a series of straps. Reggie had eaten his head clear of the sack, but the straps held his body in place and prevented him from getting his mouth on anything more.

"It's trying to blow us up?"

"It's trying to force us to land," said Nikos, back from wherever he'd been. "But I believe we will still make it to our destination." He pried himself from his gel-bed and reached for the translocational slippage engine.

"You can't use the slippage thing?"

Nikos smiled. The look of it was disturbing. "Oh yes, but not as planned."

The red representation of our vessel changed position within the device, shifting to the outside of the thing that was all inside anyway. Where it had been a new, smaller image like a insect appeared. Or maybe like a man with a pair of wings.

"You can't use that on Lorsca," I said. "He's still got Reggie!"

"Your animal will be fine. I don't have time for a proper reconfiguring to send him into a mountain, even assuming one exists on our line of longitude; your world is mostly water."

"You're not sending them to Veracruz!"

"No, that would only prevent us from going there. But I can reverse one of the fields and create an antipodean slippage."

"A what?"

"A destination point on the other side of your world."

The Svenkali chose that moment to launch its bazooka again. Nicole dropped and spun the ship with sickening speed but we were too close and the missile struck hard.

"We're going to have trouble staying aloft soon," said Nicole.

"Powering up," said Nikos.

A blurry effect that was half heat shimmer / half oil slick encompassed the Svenkali, its bazooka and wings, and my buffalito. An instant later, the field and all it contained had vanished.

"Where are they?

"Your Indian Ocean, roughly midway between South Africa and Australia."

"I can't keep us within the critical altitude much longer," said Nicole.

"You won't have to. We have sufficient charge for another use. A moment while I reconfigure..."

As Nikos applied himself, the light representing the ship floated back within the belly of the device.

"Make it half a moment."

"Powering now——"

I had the sudden feeling like I was going to be sick in two places at the same time, and then it passed, only to be replaced by a more familiar nausea as we began to fall out of the sky.

"Not to worry," called Nicole. "This is mostly a controlled

descent. I'm just getting us down before Mexican Air Traffic Control notices us and starts asking questions. We're coming in over the heart of the city. I could put us down on highway one-forty if we want."

"No need," said Nikos. "Mr. Sho has arranged a landing spot for us on the dock in front of one of his warehouses."

"A bit more difficult, but doable. Hold on tight."

We proceeded to fall out of the sky.

We set down hard between a row of cargo containers. It was still that special dark time after midnight and before dawn, which if you have to make an unannounced landing on a dock at the busiest port in the Mexican state of Veracruz, you couldn't pick a better time this side of never.

"I didn't have time to worry about sound effects or flying in like a plane would," said Nicole as we peeled ourselves from our respective gel-beds. At her command, the hatch opened. Nikos tumbled the steps out ahead of him as he exited. I followed. Nicole stayed at her board doing some final something or other with the controls.

"And here is Mr. Sho come to greet us. Ah, and someone else."

Nikos's 'someone else' was presumably the woman running towards us with a gun in her hand. She wore what was probably a standard jumpsuit for dock security, a utility belt, and boots. As she ran between the puddles of light cast by the floods mounted on the nearby warehouses I couldn't make out the actual color of her clothes, but the occasional glint of a badge on her chest — along with the gun — had me pretty confident of her job. She passed Sho, shouting at us in Spanish all the while. Her words roared by too fast for me to follow with my limited command of the language, but that was fine. I could guess what they meant and besides, the gun spoke clearly enough. I froze just outside the Uary ship, held my hands above my head, and did my best to look innocent of, well, everything.

"No hay una problema," said Mr. Sho as he caught up. "Son mis invitados."

The security guard stopped but she didn't lower her weapon. Nikos stepped forward, hand outstretched, all smiles as if he hadn't noticed the gun aimed at him, either because he was oblivious or that it happened so often he couldn't be bothered.

"Señor Sho, thank you. My apologies for any complications our abrupt arrival has caused. May I present Mr. Conroy? He is the hypnotist I told you about."

"A pleasure to make your acquaintance, Mr. Conroy."

The guard holstered her weapon and I took that as my cue to lower my arms and step forward. Although he'd just spoken fluent Spanish to the guard, the man didn't strike me as a Latino, let alone the descendant of a Mayan priest. If his English had an accent, it was the kind picked up from attending a business school in the American northeast. He was tall and skinny, and moved in that awkward gawky way of the physically self-conscious. Even in the poor light I could tell he was pale. Only the utter blackness of his straight black hair hinted at his heritage, and even that was a bit of conjecture as he wore it in a short businessman's cut.

"Likewise, I'm sure. So, um… sorghum?"

He smiled at me, his teeth gleaming and straight. "All around us. In all of these containers. This species grows only here in Mexico, and has proven resistant to several diseases which have decimated European and American crops. Supply and demand, as they say. But that's not what brings us all together, eh?"

"I suppose not, though I still haven't agreed to anything."

Sho just blinked. Nikos nodded. "Nor have we explained everything as we promised to. But come, we have a suite at a nearby hotel and our case will seem more palatable if served with a hot breakfast."

"What about your ship?"

"Mr. Sho has generously offered us the temporary occupancy of a warehouse to use as a hanger. Nicole will stay behind to effect repairs and join us as soon as she is able."

Sho nodded and stepped away to speak with his security guard.

A moment later the guard walked off toward one of the warehouses and Sho returned.

"She'll open it up and your companion can move the vessel inside. I have a car waiting to take us to the hotel, and I can send it back for her to so she can join us when she's completed her work. I'm told you have an appreciation of fine food, Mr. Conroy."

"I'm told that's something we share, Mr. Sho."

"Yes and no. I enjoy an excellent meal, but my highest appreciation is in understanding the components and the process that produces it."

"Hence your interest in cookbooks?"

"Exactly. That's the bait our friends here have used to hook me. They have promised me access to thousands of recipes that no one from Earth has ever seen. I hope to adapt them to human materials and palates. Perhaps we will get a chance to sample some of them together."

"So you're a chef as well?"

"Me? My word, no. But I am old friends with the chef at the El Presidente. He's the finest in the state, and has always been interested in whatever obscure recipe I've brought him in the past. He's also the reason why the Uary have a suite there."

Nikos had been nodding to himself during all of this, presumably letting the humans get acquainted. He jumped in now to suggest we adjourn to the hotel as planned, and Sho excused himself to alert his driver we would be leaving. As he walked away I confronted Nikos.

"Okay, so I understand Sho's motivation for your little experiment. What do I get out of it?"

The Uary smiled again. "Patience, Mr. Conroy. Patience and breakfast."

The El Presidente had been built just three decades prior, but with the look and feel of a grand hotel from two hundred years ago, a blend of 19th century Spanish splendor and native charm, all while quietly equipped with the technologies of modern life. Our driver dropped us off at the front entrance just as dawn was breaking, and Nikos led the way to a spacious set of rooms on one of the hotel's upper floors. Sho took it upon himself to call down to the kitchen for room service and I used the opportunity to freshen up. Something I'd been intending to do since before Nicole had snagged me after my show.

It's the routine moments amidst chaos that grounds us, and as I splashed water on my face and experienced the fluffiness of the El Presidente's towels, one thing rang out over the absurdity of groupmind aliens, spaceships disguised as planes, billion year racial feuds, and ancient calendrical systems: Reggie had been taken.

In my travels, I've discovered it's best to just accept the chaos that the universe can throw at you, rolling with the cosmic punches and all that. But I draw the line at people harming the handful of things that are important to me, and my buffalito stands at the head of that list. I'd cooperate with the Uary for no other reason than to be present when the Svenkali assassin put in its next appearance with Reggie along as witness, but over and beyond their own goals and purposes, I would have an accounting.

I returned to find that either I'd taken longer than I'd imagined or that the hotel staff was just that good. Nikos and Juan Sho were sitting down at a wheeled table spread with a white linen cloth and crowded with an array of covered plates and place service for four.

Nikos waved me to a seat. "Excellent timing, Mr. Conroy. Please, fill a plate and I will begin to fill your ears."

"Excuse me?"

"Your payment," he said and held out a hand, palm up, to reveal a pair of simple silver rings. Sho grinned and selected one, placing it immediately on the middle finger of his right hand. I took the remaining ring and let it rest on my palm; too heavy to be silver.

"Platinum?" I said.

The Uary shook his head and gestured at Sho as he turned to me. "Not actually, nor is either of them really a ring. These devices are composed of interlocking nanoids possessing a platinum chitin that facilitates signal transfer at the necessary speeds as well as providing a surprisingly good interface with a wide range of sapients, humans included."

"I have no idea what any of that means."

"They're to help you with your hypnotic regression."

"Okay, you need to understand something. Hypnotic regression, it doesn't work like you think it does. It has therapeutic value in some cases, but as a metaphor to help a hypnosis client get in touch with different aspects of their personality and potential. They don't actually tap into past lives. And even those who claim to be able to do that, they're talking about reincarnation of the spirit, not direct biological lineage like you're after."

Nikos was giving me that broad grin of his again. "We know that, Mr. Conroy. We understand that the hypnotic regression is only a psychological component. Thus, we add the rings." He pointed to the one I held.

"And how is it going to help me to regress Mr. Sho?"

"His ring is busy cataloging his genetic provenance and correlating the string of his ancestors with markers that exist in the field of memory and personality that the Svenkali are able to tap into with nothing more than a unique name. After you have established the hypnotic trance, Mr. Sho has agreed to our injecting him with a drug that will facilitate access to his racial memories. At that point, you will attempt to recreate the technique Kwarum Sivtinzi Lapalla used with you. Your ring will link with the identifying information from Mr. Sho's ring and make it available to your own nervous system, which will then guide his chemically primed consciousness. We believe the combination of factors will allow you to temporarily grant him access to the ancestor with whom we wish to speak, so we can learn the origin of their calendrical system."

I shook my head. "Channeling my dead aunt was a one-time event. Kwarum doubted I could do it again. And I've tried it a few times in the years since, but without results."

"I know this," said Nikos. "I was on Hesnarj because of Kwarum. He thought it was a place likely to be free of other Svenkali, as they have no use for sharing planets — let alone eternal resting places — with other races. Having already been ostracized by his people, he was working with the Uary to explore other possible ways to ensure some portion of him would endure after his death. We met several times, our last was shortly after your own encounter with him. He revealed to me that humans are one of the galaxy's few races that can manage the Svenkali trick of channeling the dead, even if only once or twice. Since then, the Uary have been exploring ways to expand that possibility. These rings are the prototype of our efforts, and yours also serves as payment. The Uary believes there is a high probability that success will reactivate your ability."

"Don't be so skeptical, Mr. Conroy," said Juan Sho. "They told me you encountered aliens on a regular basis in your career. This can't be your first time running into Clarke's second law."

I frowned. Ever since the end of the Mayan calendar and the realization that the galaxy was a lot smaller and more interesting than we'd ever dreamt, science fiction had experienced a renaissance. I'd read my share, but the hard science variety hadn't really appealed to me. I vaguely remembered Clarke as a name associated with early satellites and Sri Lanka and some rules that people invoked every time an alien race showed up with something new and shiny.

"Was that the one about unfamiliar technology looking like magic?" I asked.

"That's the third law. The second says, 'The only way of discovering the limits of the possible is to venture a little way past them into the impossible.'"

I turned to Nikos. "Is that what we're doing, venturing into the impossible?"

He spread his hands in an all too human gesture. "It is fair to say that nothing like this has been attempted before, Mr. Conroy. But such efforts and pursuits are a common part of Uary existence."

Nicole arrived just as we were finishing breakfast.

"Did anyone see you come here?" I asked.

"I think so. I made several stops along the way and did my best to leave a clear trail."

I was halfway across the room towards her with no clear idea what I intended to do once I reached her but she brought me up short with a raised hand and the words, "You do want your buffalito back, don't you?"

Nikos stood. "We have a plan, you know."

She nodded. "A simple trap. A sequence of stun grenades that will trigger after Lorsca enters the suite, a sufficient quantity to leave it incapacitated for thirty hours. More than enough time for us to complete the project and depart."

"How does that get me Reggie?"

"Our assassin will have Reggie with it when it arrives here," she said.

"And be on the receiving end of thirty hours worth of stun!"

"Mr. Conroy, there are few things in the galaxy more durable than an Arconi buffalo dog. Even assuming your pet succumbs to the stun, the worst effect he will experience is a period of unconsciousness."

"And then what?"

"After we have left you can come here and collect your animal. Even if Lorsca has awakened, you'll have nothing to fear; you are not among its targets. And we will have moved on."

"Why not come back yourselves, and deal with it once and for all? Why keep running?"

Nikos joined Nicole at the door and as I looked into his eyes I could truly believe he was eighteen hundred years old.

"The Uary is incapable of violence, Mr. Conroy. Each of us is part of a vaster archive than exists anywhere else in our galaxy, but I can no more cause harm to another sapient being than you can engage in dialogue with the cells of your body. Not even to one who has dedicated its long life to eradicating my kind. We cannot defeat the Svenkali, we can only escape it for a time and continue our work."

"Would you care for something to eat first?" asked Juan Sho.

Nicole smiled and shook her head. "Thank you, no. I obtained a light meal at one of my stops. Now, if you please, a cab, the first of several, is waiting for us downstairs."

'Several cabs' turned out to be eight. We'd exit from one and as soon as it drove off Nicole or Nikos would hail another and we'd continue on. We crisscrossed the city of Veracruz several times in this way. I suppose if I had an assassin who would stop at nothing to track and kill me that I'd be paranoid too. Then again, it's not paranoia when someone's really after you.

We finally arrived at what was basically a private park. Nicole had somehow arranged the use of a vast bit of green space kept clear in the middle of a small forest on the estate of some wealthy and powerful personage in Veracruz.

The Uary believed that a natural setting would facilitate what we were attempting. Tall trees surrounded us on all sides, hiding the buildings of the land's owner. The eighth cab had dropped us off at a locked gate that had yielded to a series of codes Nicole had ready. We entered the estate, walked a good quarter mile down a dirt drive, and then angled off into the adjacent trees.

After about five minutes of walking through the woods, we passed a small relay station, one of a dozen which, according to Nicole, defined an early alert sensory ring. She tapped out a sequence on her padd, activating the device as we passed within its perimeter, and ran a diagnostic. We kept walking until we left the trees behind and reached the center of a glade. If anything intended to disturb us, the sensory ring would let us know, and even if that failed we'd see it coming.

In addition to her padd, Nicole and Nikos both carried large wicker baskets of assorted gear, including additional food and drink, the first hint of how long their endeavor might take. We settled in as for a picnic. Juan Sho and I sat across from one another on a blanket Nicole spread for us on the grass. Then she and Nikos sat behind Sho, silent and immobile and out of his view. The Uary nodded to me in unison. I thought about Reggie, wondered if he were scared or just taking it all in stride, if the Svenkali saw him as a living being that it should feel responsibility for, or more like an inanimate object that it needed to bring along as it finished its mission. Either way, I couldn't do a thing about it. I nodded to Sho.

"Are you ready?"

He grinned at me, his weak chin aquiver with excitement. "I've never been more ready in my life. In a couple hours I'm going to have access to recipes no other human being has seen. Let's do this."

"That's fine. Just relax. Rest your hands lightly in your lap. Take a deep breath in, hold it, that's right, now let it out. Bring your eyes to mine, focus on them, and let the world around us fade from your awareness…"

I continued with a straightforward induction, keeping the tone of things light but not flashy; no snappy patter or clever quips. This wasn't a stage show and my goal wasn't entertainment. Sho slipped into a light trance without resistance and in short order I took him considerably deeper.

I nodded to Nikos who soundlessly rose to his feet, coming forward to hover just above Juan Sho. He'd taken a pressure hypo from one of the baskets and now applied the business end to my subject's neck. The sorghum executive winced but did not otherwise react or awaken. So far, so good.

Deeper and deeper I guided Sho into his trance, blocking out all other frames of reference or competing stimuli. My voice was the only thing in his entire world, the source of everything that existed. I took him down to the point where I could instruct him to regress, reach back, and begin to confabulate past lives.

But it wasn't going to be like that. I took his hands lightly in mine, holding them so that our rings touched.

"Juan Sho, we are going to go on a voyage now, not of distance but of time. We are traveling backwards down your family tree. As we slide, from one ancestor to the next, you will briefly experience that life. With each generation you will find the connection growing stronger. Do you understand?"

"Yes."

"Let go of your sense of self, and merge with the memory of your father. You know the man, you can feel him inside you as we step backwards in time."

Deep in his trance Sho murmured. "I'm my father."

"Very good. Now we're letting go again. That was just a stop on the way. Let go of your father's memories and slip back another generation. Your grandfather's memories are all around you. Reach out, wrap them close."

"We're in Guatemala," said Sho.

"Your grandfather is in Guatemala?"

"Yes. My grandfather. And you."

Pronouns are funny. I hadn't intended it, but Sho was taking me along with him. No problem. One of the first things I learned as a stage performer is to work with whatever your subject gives you. There are no glitches, only unplanned features.

"That's right. I'm there because I'm your guide on this journey. I'm going to introduce you to many people. Now, let go of your grandfather's memories, and reach back still further to his father. Rise up through them like a diver swimming upwards to break the water's surface. The water is his memory, his sense of self. And it is vast, deep as a mountain lake. It doesn't matter where your surface, you are somewhere in his life's memory."

"Yes, that's true. I am."

"Where are you? What are you doing?"

"I am carving."

"What are you carving?"

"Puppets. I am carving puppets. For my son's birthday. We are having a party. Will you come too?"

"I'd be delighted. But wait, it's time to move on. This too was just a stop for us. Let go, dive down again, plunge deeper. Reach back again, and slip to his father's memories and find yourself surfacing again a generation further back..."

I continued like this, slowly easing him along a patrilineal line of ancestors, and each time Sho's mind added me to the scene. I wondered what he thought of me, an eternal friend of his father's side of the family, always present in every generation. It had to be eerie.

Sho became more adept at leaping into one ancestor after another, but even so it was slow going. Out of the corner of my eye I could see Nicole had moved closer. She held her padd in one hand and a stylus in the other, taking notes and checking off each generation as we eased backward.

After two hours, I had guided him back through eighty-nine generations. More grandfathers than would fit in our suite back at the El Presidente had been invoked and then sent on their way. Through it all Sho had responded in English, a language most of his ancestors couldn't have known. How then, could the Uary believe him to be truly regressing into the memories of earlier generations when all the while he retained a fluent command of a language that should have long ceased being his native tongue?

"Very good, Mr. Conroy," said Nicole. "Now we can ask him."

"I don't think so. You said your drug made him more sensitive to racial memory, whatever that means, but I don't think you've got the real deal here."

She gave a knowing — and perhaps somewhat condescending — smile. "The drug was what allowed him to follow your instructions, to track his lineage back generation through generation, nothing more. Does he not believe he is his ancestor? Does he not know with a certainty that he is a high priest of the Mayan people?"

"Yeah, that's all true as far as it goes, but that's only because he's so suggestible. He's going along with what he's been told, and he may even believe it, but it's all confabulation."

"Oh, we understand that," said Nikos. "But that is why you are here, Mr. Conroy. His belief, however false, is still solid in his mind. Think of it as a clearing."

"What do you mean, a clearing?"

"A clearing for the real thing," said Nicole. "A space in his mind and personality that calls to the ancestor we wish to question, that is shaped to that one individual. And now, if you are ready, we want you to use the technique you acquired from the

Svenkali to invoke Mr. Sho's ancestor, and land him in this clearing."

Right. This was the big moment, the real reason the Uary had come to me. The alien who taught me had been banished from the speaking of the Svenkali for having channeled a sentient being of another race long before meeting me. I was possibly the only non-Svenkali in existence who had done this thing. I nodded to the Uary and closed my eyes. I gathered my thoughts and memories of that one experience eighteen years ago. The feeling in my mind had been chaotic back then. Kwarum had imposed structure, requiring me to say the full name of the person I wished to invoke.

The Uary did not know the name of their ancient Mayan priest, but the ring on my hand had been feeding my mind with details of Sho's ancestor, the identity confirmed from ancient DNA and traced forward to where it resided in this unlikely descendant whom I'd hypnotized.

It may have been that trancing Sho had heightened my own suggestibility, but I *knew* that ancient Mayan priest, name or no name. It didn't matter that nearly two thousand years separated him from Sho. Nor that the memories were confabulated, nor that they lacked a common language. Sho's ring had done its job. He held in his mind a certainty that he had become that long vanished man. That confidence, backed by the sensitivity to genetic markers that the Uary's drug had achieved, conspired with my own efforts, sparking an ability that I had come to view as a one-shot gift, not likely to be repeated.

I could feel the changes in my mind, like a forgotten arroyo suddenly awash and flowing again.

I reached out, beyond the constraints of distance and time, and touched that immeasurable energy field of sentience that lies beyond death, tapping it as the Svenkali can, as I had managed once before. The Mayan priest came to me, and for a moment his entire life's experiences took up residence in my mind.

And then, just as quickly as he had arrived he fled, passing from me through the connections of our rings and into the body of Juan Sho. I felt blown apart, a dandelion gone to seed and scattered helplessly by a spring wind. Every trace of the priest vanished from me, and with it much of myself as well. I slumped sideways onto the grass, my eyes too tired to close.

From far off I heard a faint yapping sound, but I knew it couldn't be real, just wishful thinking borne out of a combination of exhaustion and altered awareness. Much as I wanted Reggie to be here and safe with me, that wasn't the situation. I pushed away from the hallucination, much like a square-dancer ridding himself of a unwanted partner, hoping the metaphor would hold and propel me into the arms of the real world. One of my cheeks tingled; individual blades of grass called my name. I dismissed the name-calling as a product of overactive imagination and figurative language, but I welcomed its source. Grass on my face brought the world back. Sitting up struck me as a wonderful idea, and one that I intended to pursue on some future occasion when my body seemed more inclined to listen to me.

"Mr. Conroy! Mr. Conroy! What has happened?"

I opened my eyes to find Nicole hovering over me. She looked concerned, though not necessarily about me.

"It's okay," I said, my words weak and slurred. "It's done."

"Done?" said Nikos. "You mean you have summoned the priest?"

"Yeah, but you'd better talk to him now. I don't know how long it will last." With eternal patience and glacial speed I let my eyes close. Nikos and Nicole started making funny noises. Some auditory hallucination brought on by exhaustion and the changes in my brain chemistry, but no, surely they were just speaking another language. I wondered how they'd learned it. Did they have ancient Mayan in their shared memory?

The Uary spoke slowly, voices calm and soft, taking turns in a way that probably felt natural to them but would have had me turning my head from one to the other, generating me a stiff neck and unconscious resentment. If it hit Sho's ancestor that way I couldn't tell. He hadn't spoken yet, but that didn't surprise me. He had a lot to take in. Nicole was patiently explaining something to him when he interrupted and spoke for the first time. Nikos laughed.

"What's so funny?" I said, not even trying to open my eyes again. My words took twice as long to produce as they should have. Even my tongue was tired. "I thought you had serious things to talk about."

"He says he knows you," said Nikos.

"Knows me?"

"He says you are a god who has shown him all the children of his future. He believes that we are your priests, and that all of this was foretold, that we are all due the honor and glory of sacrifice."

"Yeah, well, thank him for the honor, but I'm too tired for ceremonies. Tell him I'm a tired god." Nikos and Nicole resumed their questioning of the Mayan priest.

He began answering them, slowly at first, somewhat slurred and confused, which may have been the trance and may have been the unfamiliarity of his twenty-first century mouth forming sounds and sequences it had no practice with. He picked it up quickly though, and started responding more rapidly.

In hindsight, having my eyes closed made all the difference. Had they been open, the added sensory input might have prevented me from hearing the faint, high-pitched whistle amidst the babble of a Mayan dialect not spoken aloud in centuries. But I did hear it, coming from above us, and noticed it growing louder. I looked up into a bright blue sky, empty except for a few fluffy white clouds and a tiny mote that grew larger as I watched. The mote expanded to a speck, the speck to a dot, and the dot to a pebble, and that last comparison pushed some switch in my weary brain. I wanted to stand but my legs wouldn't work. I had to settle for sitting up.

Nicole broke off from her conversation with the priest. "Mr. Conroy, what's wrong?"

I'd never been more tired, and more than a little loopy. My life was draining away and suddenly all I could think about was the pretty Uary next door being decanted or hatched or whatever decades back in the 20th century. "Your boyfriend's back, and there's going to be trouble."

"My... boyfriend?"

I couldn't lift my arm. I let my head drop back, pointing to the sky with my chin. Whether she realized what I was doing or finally registered the whistling sound, she looked up. Me too. The unidentifiable pebble had grown to become a humanoid silhouette plunging toward us at great speed.

"What's the whistling?" My head felt clearer; maybe it was adrenaline, maybe I was recovering. Either way, the sentence came more easily to my lips.

Nikos and Sho's ancestor had stopped talking. Both stared up at the plummeting figure. Nikos did that thing with his eyes that I'd seen the Uary do before. They returned to normal a second later.

"Aero-skis," he said.

"Aero-skis?"

"A Clarkeson recreational product. The technology should not be available on Earth."

"Kind of like your longitudinal slippage thingamajig?"

Nicole frowned as my point registered. "Indeed. Our data-broker would seem to also be supplying our adversary. How very duplicitous."

The Uary might occupy a niche as the galaxy's oldest librarians, but they were also proving themselves naïve. "Isn't that the very definition of a Clarkeson?"

Nikos frowned at me. "Aero-skis are not approved technology for this world. The Clarkeson's sale of them would violate several trade agreements and the third seeker's possession would carry criminal charges."

"Yeah... I think you have more pressing worries when it comes to your boy, Lorsca."

As if I'd conjured it with its name, the airborne figure drew close enough to resolve into a Svenkali. At this distance I could make out a pair of nearly transparent objects bound to its feet, sized more like individual snowboards than skis. The whistling had grown in volume, assaulting our ears now like a banshee wailing of impending death. Yes, my brain was serving up all sorts of helpful imagery.

Juan Sho had stood up and spread his arms in the direction of the falling figure. He shouted and gestured and I had no idea what he was saying, but the Uary did. They turned to him, and began arguing about... something. Meanwhile the Svenkali on its aero-skis had begun braking. Nikos's advance warning sensors never went off, not even when Lorsca swooped down to our level and barreled into both Uary and Sho, knocking all three of them off their feet.

Lorsca's skis dissolved or retracted or maybe simply splintered off on impact. It stood with feet planted firmly in the grass, one arm raised high above its head, holding a shiny new peeler in its hand. The weapon glinted in the sun, a blue to match the sky. Across the Svenkali's torso my buffalito squirmed in a mesh sack, his furry head sticking out the top as before, but just like last time several bands pinned his body in place and prevented him from eating his way free. His eyes locked on mine and he barked with what I hoped was not misplaced relief.

The assassin looked over our little picnic, took a step, and with no hesitation kicked Nicole in the head. Then, with its other hand it reached down and hauled Nikos to his feet. The Uary hung like an unstrung puppet.

"I am Lorsca, third seeker on the path. You have hidden among others, but you cannot disguise your true self from my mission. You are the Uary. Eight hundred and fourteen Uary have I corrected. Today that number grows. I identify you as your kind have named themselves since the moment of your first, unforgivable offense. Acknowledge this truth as your last fact and I will end you more swiftly than you deserve."

The setting had changed, and there were more players on the stage, but this was definitely where I had come in.

Juan Sho — or rather the newly reincarnated Mayan priest I'd helped awaken within his body — started shouting. I still couldn't understand what he was saying, but outrage sounds the same in any language. He'd risen to a crouch after being knocked down by the Svenkali's landing. He gestured to me, called something, an instruction, an insult, I don't know. I remembered the Uary explaining that the priest had called me a god. Then his gaze moved back to Lorsca and widened still more as he saw the bison-like face of Reggie poking out of it just below its collarbone.

Reggie didn't like the attention and barked at Sho. More of the lethargy from our experiment was fading away and I surged up onto my knees.

Sho's eyes lingered a moment longer then darted to Nicole sprawled nearest to him, and then over to Nikos dangling from the Svenkali's outstretched hand.

Nikos began speaking, faint mewling sounds of an alien tongue that may have been a string of demands or a refutation of everything the Svenkali stood for, but sounded like pleading. Lorsca ignored them and shook the Uary. "There is a witness, and you will speak the words in his language. Now."

He took a breath and switched to English. "I am the Uary. I am no threat to you, but you will do as you will do."

"I will," said Lorsca.

"No!" I screamed that one syllable, and the effort made me think my brain would hemorrhage or my heart explode. Neither happened but my hand burned with a cold that ran up my arm and across my chest. My hand.

I spent an eternity bringing my left hand to the middle finger of my right. I pulled at the Uary's ring, tearing flesh as I forced it off my finger and flung it at the Svenkali.

He stood less than two meters from me, but my throw had no strength and it landed at Lorsca's feet. My buffalo dog's eyes followed the arc like I had initiated a game of fetch and cruel fate kept him from playing.

Whether a function of my shout, the ring, or Reggie's sudden petulant whining, the Svenkali's attention broke for an instant. The peeler it'd been bringing down toward Nikos's throat paused.

In that moment, the priest acted. He scooped up Nicole's padd's stylus from where it had fallen in the grass and leapt at the Svenkali. He stabbed at its chest, slashing one of the bands that pinned my buffalito. Sho's free hand grappled with Lorsca's hand holding the peeler. The assassin maintained its grip on Nikos, but that was about all it could do. The priest possessing Sho's body, the two aliens, and my buffalo dog fell in a heap. An instant later, Reggie squirmed free and bounded toward me while the others tumbled over one another in the grass, wrestling and writhing. Reggie barreled into me and it required all of my energy to hold him and not pitch over again. I curled my fingers tightly in his fur, my eyes locked on the trio just beyond my reach.

And then all movement stopped.

Sho sat up, a wild look in his eyes. One hand still held Lorsca's wrist, and had brought the Svenkali's own weapon to its neck. A gash had blossomed like a pebbly chrysanthemum stump. Lorsca's severed head lay half a meter beyond.

The priest's other hand still gripped the stylus and had slammed it into Nikos's chest just slightly left of center. As I watched he let the Svenkali's arm fall away and brought both hands together to yank the stylus further to the side tearing the flesh, up and then down, until he'd made enough room to release the implement and plunge his hand into the cavity.

What little fluid seeped from the gaping wound looked more like thick orange syrup than blood. Surprise flooded across Nikos's face even as his pallor blanched. He gasped soundlessly. Nicole had sat up, screamed once, and gone catatonic. I had the feeling that I should be vomiting at the sight, if only I wasn't so tired. But the strangest expression was worn by Sho's channeled priest. He looked stricken and fearful. His hand pulled free of Nikos's chest, holding what appeared to be a cluster of bright orange grapes. I recalled the Uary's earlier words about sacrifice. Sho had gone looking for a heart and found something else, something he couldn't understand.

Reggie resumed barking. My exhaustion had begun to dissipate once I'd thrown away the ring. I staggered to my feet, desperate for something to do before the priest decided to try his game of organ show-and-tell on anyone else.

I stumbled closer, letting gravity pull me back down to my knees, one hand dropping to Sho's shoulder to break my fall and get his attention. I knelt among two alien corpses and the murdering Mayan priest I'd hypnotically reincarnated. I locked my gaze with him and we swayed together for a moment as I caught my breath.

Taking that moment was a mistake. Without looking away from me he drew the stylus from Nikos's body and jammed it into my chest even as I issued a command.

"Sleep!"

He collapsed, tumbling backwards to the grass.

If I'd said it a few seconds sooner I might have been able to stand up and check on Nicole. As it was, I'd been stabbed in the chest and my body decided the best course of action was for me to collapse as well. I sprawled across the decapitated Svenkali and the gutted Uary and the world went away.

Consciousness returned in stages. I had a sense of being flat on my back and a clear realization that I couldn't move. Proprioception informed me that my legs lay stretched out with my feet slightly apart. My arms were by my sides and my hands were turned downward. Grass tickled my palms and the back of my neck. I had a dull pain in my chest. I remembered Juan Sho stabbing me, and that was sufficient to pull me the rest of the way to wakefulness. I opened my eyes and immediately wished I hadn't.

A purple and pimply face loomed over me, though calling it a face required equal parts charity and imagination. The visage lacked traditional sensory organs and it looked more like a brain than a face, organized into lobes by a series of vertical sulci that oozed some vaguely transparent gunk. It attached via a neck of raw, ringed muscle that in turn flowed into a torso of what I can only describe as tiger-striped gelatin. For good or ill this apparition appeared only half naked; from the waist down it wore avocado slacks that reminded me of the ones Nikos had been wearing. Nikos, who had not only also been stabbed, but eviscerated before my eyes. Had this creature stolen the Uary's pants for its own use?

I tried to get away. I wanted to crawl, scramble, run. I was all about the flight; the fight option never popped into my brain. Which would have been swell except I couldn't move. Nor could I scream or plead or call for help. The monster that had stolen Nikos's pants waggled one of its hands over my face, revealing seven spatulated digits somewhere between fingers and tendrils. Each of these was capped with a disc of bluish metal. Its other hand cupped something that I recognized as Nicole's padd, and as it waggled the one hand over me its attention was rooted on the object in its other. I should mention that in all my traveling I'd never seen an alien that looked even remotely like this thing, nor had I ever heard a matching description. We're talking alien even by alien standards.

I heard a familiar bark and Juan Sho's face entered my field of vision. He stood above and behind the weird creature, holding my buffalito with both hands. He smiled down at me and an instant after he set Reggie on the ground I was on the receiving end of a massive face washing with a generous side of extra slobber. That continued for a couple minutes and, despite the horror hovering above me, went a long way to calming my nerves.

When my buffalito felt reassured enough to ease up on the face-licking, I turned my attention back to Sho. He had some blood on his shirt which was probably mine, as well as a generous splash of that orange syrup that Nikos had very thoughtfully previously kept inside his body. I assumed that Sho's stylus wielding ancestor had faded or fled and the sorghum magnate was himself again. He knelt on the other side of me from Reggie, one hand aiming for my face, and tapped something that had been placed on my forehead while I'd been unconscious. At that touch, I experienced a sensation like water rushing off your skin when you sit up in a bathtub. The paralysis that had kept me silent fell away, taking my panic with it and leaving behind a sense of well-being. Knowing it was artificial didn't dampen its effect one bit.

"Hey, Juan," I muttered through the euphoric haze. A string of mellow questions flittered through me, several of them involving whatever he'd touched on my forehead that had me so dopey.

"Shh, try not to move. Nikos is almost done. He's tending to the last little cosmetic bits now. He says you won't even have a scar."

Nikos? I glanced again at Mr. Purple Brainface. Nikos? No, he was dead, surely. And this thing had taken his pants. I flipped Occam's razor back and forth a few times over that one. Which was the simpler answer: that Nikos had survived — despite Sho's ancestor gutting him like a trout — and turned into the creature looming above me, or that a monster had showed up after all the other impossible events of the day and helped itself to the dead alien's pants?

I couldn't make up my mind so I opted to go with Sho's implied version. At least for the moment. That and the fact that Reggie was so happy to see me and not barking at or trying to protect me from the monster.

"I saw you die," I said to the thing, but then amended. "Sho ripped your heart out."

Laughter bubbled up from several sulci; literally bubbled. I felt like I might be sick.

"That wasn't my heart," said the creature. "It was a much less critical organ, my adaptation cluster. Not that I won't miss it." Its speech had the same contours as Nikos's, but the voice was off, more raspy and higher. "Your concern is touching, though."

I closed my eyes, did a mental count from one to five, and opened them again. Nope. Same oozing brain face.

"Adaptation cluster?"

"Yes, Mr. Conroy. Without it my body has reverted to its true form."

"That's what you guys really look like?"

"We are archivists and data collectors," said the monster that I had to admit was really Nikos. "We have to be able to mingle with other races, to walk among them without detection. Each nodule of the cluster contains thousands of physiognomic sequences. Selecting the right combination allows the Uary to express an appearance consistent with nearly any of the intelligent races in our galaxy."

"So having those, um, nodules cut out wasn't a mortal injury."

"Precisely. I was extremely fortunate. A few centimeters to either side and Mr. Sho could have plucked out something vital."

Nikos set down the padd and then began plucking the metal caps off from his fingertips. When finished, he tapped the object on my forehead and lifted it off. The pain in my chest had already faded and the euphoria followed after.

Nikos stepped back. "That should do it."

Reggie jumped into my lap as I sat up and I cradled him with both hands. All was right with the world again.

Well, sort of. A quick glance around showed the grape-like cluster that had been inside Nikos, Lorsca's severed head, and a bit further away the rest of the Svenkali's body.

"Where's Nicole?"

"She's gone to retrieve our vessel," said Nikos. "I'm a bit too conspicuous now to simply walk out of here, and there's plenty of room in the glade for her to land."

"So you're done and cutting your losses?" I said.

If Nikos frowned at me, I couldn't tell. "Not every venture can succeed, Mr. Conroy. We sought to learn two new things: Whether we could approximate the Svenkali ability to access the personae and knowledge of those who have experienced mortal death, as well as how your ancient Mayans came to know the future date that your planet would experience contact."

"And?"

He held up a pair of rings, the one Juan Sho had worn as well as the one I had ripped from my hand and thrown away. "A detailed analysis will be done, but the early data from these devices suggest that our limited success today was only possible because you had already previous experienced the process. The potential may exist in all humans, but without a Svenkali to quicken it, we cannot replicate it ourselves."

I nodded and kept the relief from my face. No need to let the

Uary know that I didn't think the galaxy was ready for a planet of human beings all able to talk to their own or anyone else's dead.

"And the calendar thing?"

"We fared a bit better there, but even so the answer was incomplete. Mr. Sho's ancestor was able to tell us of holy knowledge passed along only to high priests. He spoke of a dead god with bright hair and many voices who came to his own ancestors with a prophecy that time was like a great wheel, and that only years after the wheel had completed its turning would all debts be paid."

"Cryptic," I said.

Nikos nodded his big purple-brained head. "Indeed. And not particularly illuminated. We can surmise that the calendrical system came from an extraterrestrial visitor, but even so we still do not know how this 'dead god' knew the future."

Juan Sho had been gathering up the bits of equipment scattered by Lorsca' s attack, piling everything onto the blanket we had used. As Nikos finished speaking he joined us, shaking his head.

"But that's not all of it. That's what he told you, but he was hesitating, holding stuff back."

"Mr. Sho?"

"He was in my head. I remember what he said, and what he was thinking. Some of it doesn't make sense, and maybe that's because it wasn't in English and while I could understand him it doesn't really translate all that well."

"What did he leave out?" I asked.

"Details," said Sho. "Like why the dead god was called the dead god."

"Why?"

"Its skin was dead white, like a bloodless corpse. It came to them naked, and had no genitals."

"And the many voices?" I asked.

"It was a lot more than many. The number had been passed down from priest to priest. One million, eight hundred seventy-two thousand separate voices, all speaking as one."

"That's a very precise number," I said.

"It's part of the Mayan calendar, the number of days in a Long

Count cycle of thirteen baktuns. The last day of the last baktun marked the date of Galactic Contact."

Nikos sat down suddenly, burying his purply head in his spatulated hands.

"Problem?" I asked.

"I had not put the pieces together. The Uary had them but never saw the connection."

"What connection?"

He lowered his hands. "The Uary has of course known the number of days in the Long Count. As you said, it is a precise number, but not a unique one. It is also the number of separate, self-aware committees that come together to form a functioning Clarkeson."

"Corpselike skin," I repeated. "And brightly-colored hair."

Nikos nodded.

"You're saying the 'dead god' that gave the Mayans their calendar was a Clarkeson? Then what's the bit about debts being paid mean?"

"He was going to tell you that piece, but that's when the Svenkali showed up. And because Mr. Conroy was here, my ancestor thought he was some kind of instrument of the prophecy. That's when it all went nuts."

"What piece? What prophecy?"

"The dead god was from the future," said Sho. "It brought the calendar and told its story so that it would be passed forward through time to all the priests. It promised that a holy duo from its own past would come seeking a priest, that they would be guided by an incredible god who showed that priest his own future's children. These three, the holy duo and their incredible god, were also from the future, but a future that was from the dead god's past. When those two pasts catch up, *that's* when the priest was to honor the dead god with the blood sacrifice of the others. That would cause all debts to be paid."

I shook my head. "I don't get it."

"Don't you see," said Nikos, despair in his voice. "The Clarkesons possess time travel."

I stared at him. "No, they don't. Time travel is impossible. Everyone knows that."

"You're right. And the Uary knows this better than anyone. The ability to interact with the past is a story that shows up in all cultures, but its reality would shatter the galaxy as we know it. It cannot exist."

"Then how do you explain Sho's ancestor's story?"

"Coincidence, nothing more." said Nikos, but it was clear he didn't believe his own words.

"And the bit about the god who would show the priest his future's children?"

"More of the same."

"An incredible god," I said.

"The Mayan had no shortage of gods," said Nikos. "I don't think superlatives matter."

"Unless it's a translation error, from whatever language Sho's ancestor spoke to modern English. Maybe it wasn't 'incredible' at all. Maybe the word was something else entirely."

"Such as?"

I shrugged. "Amazing?"

"Yes. Even you see it."

"Excuse me?"

"The Uary is a collection of archivists, Mr. Conroy. Each of us exists to contribute to the collective knowledge of the whole. We automatically share with all the Uary, thirty times each day. Moreover, unlike the Svenkali, we spread that knowledge, all of it, to other races throughout the galaxy."

"Can't you hold information back?"

Nikos shook his head. "The Uary can no more censor a piece of its archive than you can choose to breathe only certain molecules of the oxygen you inhale. All of the facts have been placed before me and I cannot ignore the obvious conclusion: The Clarkesons have acquired the ability to travel back through time. Moreover, they have deliberately manipulated events so that the Uary would learn this fact, and disseminate it far and wide."

"That doesn't sound good," said Juan Sho.

"Indeed. I cannot envision a greater opposite of good than what would result. Galactic chaos. Devastation on a level the galaxy has never seen. Along with endless studies proving the impossibility of time travel, the Uary's archive contains models for what would happen if it were somehow possible. The Clarkesons know this as well."

I connected the last set of dots. "You're saying they did this deliberately?"

"It is their nature."

"And all of this was set in motion centuries ago? We've just been waiting around for events to catch up with us. We're already screwed."

Nikos lifted his head from his hands. His facial lobes pulsed. "Perhaps... not."

"How not? You know the truth, so it's part of the Uary archive now."

"Not yet. Right now, only we three know that time travel exists. The Uary sharing is cyclical and won't happen again for approximately twenty minutes. At that time, yes, the Clarkeson's plan will be complete."

"But that's *your* nature, adding to the knowledge base."

"Then we must prevent that nature. I require your assistance for this; the Uary cannot cause harm. It must be done, before Nicole returns. She must not learn any of this."

I set Reggie aside and went to see what lay on the blanket that I could use as a weapon. I found nothing, and moved on to search the Svenkali's body. "Do you need to prepare? Are there any words you need us to say?"

"All has been said. Lead Nicole to believe my injuries were not as superficial as we'd believed."

A flat square detached from the underside of Lorsca's boot. It had a pair of slits on opposite sides and a set of recessed switches on a third one. I held it at arm's length and began pressing buttons. A gleaming beam shot out from the slits to create an aero-ski. Another press and it vanished.

Sho stared at me, realization painting horror across his face. "You can't... I won't help..."

Nikos and I ignored him. If I failed, if the existence of time travel became known, someone somewhen would have come back to stop me. No one did.

"Thank you, Mr. Conroy."

I stood beside the Uary and held the square in front of him, one of the slit ends pressed to his chest. "You're absolutely sure about your models and projections?"

"It is the sort of thing the Uary is best at," he said.

We *all* act according to our nature. For human beings, this can mean setting aside our insistence on a better outcome and accepting the necessity of actions that will haunt us ever after. Occam's razor didn't help here; either side of the blade led to regret.

I pressed a button.

Nikos took about five minutes to die. When I retracted the aero-ski, I saw it had carved a rectangular hole though some critical organ, presumably an Uary-analog to the human heart. The wound gushed more orange syrup and his body convulsed, but he never spoke.

Juan Sho spent an additional five minutes being sick.

Nicole returned with the Uary vessel about half an hour later.

We used that time to clean up the scene a bit. I stripped the Svenkali of the rest of its equipment and fed all of it to my buffalito, then did the same with the Uary's pair of rings, and everything that Sho had piled on the blanket. With his help, I used it to wrap around Nikos like a shroud. Reggie sat next to the body, whimpering softly.

Lorsca had to do without, but I did fetch its head and set it on its chest.

When Nicole arrived her grief over Nikos's death distracted her from the lie that Reggie had gone into a feeding frenzy and devoured all our gear.

"I don't understand," she said, checking notes on the padd that she'd taken with her, the only object that had survived my buffalito's impromptu meal. "I checked him over before I left. We both reviewed the instruments' readings. Other than the loss of his adaptation cluster, he appeared fine."

"I'm sorry," I said. "If it's any consolation, he seemed to pass quickly and without pain." Sho just stared at the ground.

"This mission came first. The attempt to recreate what the Svenkali can do, that was worth everything. Honestly, neither of us expected to survive, not once we knew Lorsca had tracked us to Earth. We'd talked about it. We had a plan that whichever of us it took first, the other was to use that as an opportunity to escape and survive long enough to share what we'd learned with the rest of the Uary."

"And you've done that?" I asked.

"Shortly before my return. We know that technology cannot effectively duplicate the Svenkali's abilities. And we know that Earth was visited in its past by non-humans. Neither is quite what we'd hoped to learn, but we know more than we did before. For that, you both have the gratitude of the Uary."

I nodded to Sho. "Is there anything else we can do to help with the bodies?"

"I understand the human sentiment, and I appreciate the intention. But no, the Svenkali will realize soon enough that their seeker has died, and have no special regard for the body once life has gone. The Uary has always taken a similar, pragmatic view. I'll incinerate all the remains when we lift; the grass will grow back soon enough. Thank you for your care though. "

"So what happens now?" I asked.

"I'll take you back to Mr. Sho's dock. I've left a data storage device for him back at the El Presidente with his promised payment of recipes that have long been lost from the known galaxy. And I've spoken to the chef there. He'll be happy to prepare a feast for you both, all of his specialties. It's the least I can do for involving you in this."

I offered up a small smile. "Will there be enough for Reggie too?"

She stroked his furry head. "There'll be plenty for him. But really, what is *enough* for a buffalito?"

Some questions cannot be answered, even by the Uary. Others shouldn't be. We climbed aboard Nicole's vessel and left in pursuit of a meal.

The End

TIMELINE

WHAT HAPPENS WHEN
IN THE CONROYVERSE

1991
Fiona Katherine St. Vincent Wyndmoor is born.

2012
End of Mayan Calendar, and Humanity's first contact with extraterrestrials.

2018
Mexico shocks the world by outlawing most alien races from inside its borders.

2026
Amadeus Colson defines one edge of Human Space.

2042
The "Great Texas Temporal Disaster" – a Physics experiment at a Waco university goes awry, creating areas of slowed time.

2044
Texas loses its statehood and is removed from the United States of America.

2049

Left-John Mocker is born of Comanche parents in Oklahoma.

2057
Conroy is born!

2072
Fiona Katherine St. Vincent Wyndmoor dies and, against her family's wishes, is buried on Hesnarj.

2076
Conroy is marooned on Hesnarj and takes up hypnosis.

2079
Conroy meets Left-John Mocker at the Aztec in El Paso, Texas.

Kwarum Sivtinzi Lapalla dies, never to be named by any living Svenkali.

2089
Conroy steals a fertile buffalo dog off Gibrahl and sets up Buffalogic, Inc.

Gel acquires Barry.

2090
Left-John Mocker wins the Extra-Solar Poker Classic Tournament.

Buffalogic, Inc. lends its support to an archaeological dig near the Martian city of Seroni.

Conroy meets the Uary and hypnotically regresses an ancient Mayan priest.

2091
Conroy performs at a club and reminisces about how he became a hypnotist.

Conroy helps an unwilling telepath deal with his ability.

2092

Conroy visits Brunzibar and falls in love with the Baroness Parmaq.

Left-John Mocker wins a quarter share of the Golden Turtle Palace in Newer Jersey.

2093
Conroy plays "matter" with a telepathic Taurian.

Conroy and the Mocker visit a casino on Triton and encounter Angela Colson.

Melody Wilder begins her doctoral work on Niflheim station.

2094
Green Aggression begins its attack on Buffalogic, Inc.

The Plenum senate places Angela Colson on probation.

2095
Conroy turns himself over to the Arconi.

Angela Colson learns the secret origins of the Clarkesons.

Melody Wilder is offered the newly chair of the Department of Quilton Studies.

2096
Conroy meets Svetlana Villanova. Also Billi. And a Celestial.

2098
Conroy returns to Colson's Planet.

The novella you've just read, Trial of the Century, *leaves the Amazing Conroy free to pursue his true calling as a hypnotist throughout*

the galaxy. But to truly succeed, he's going to need something he hasn't had since he was back on Earth: an agent! It should be show business as usual, except for...

- *the energy-being the size of a hundred suns that wants to study him,*
- *a troupe of alien sex wrestlers,*
- *a bartender who can edit her customers' memory,*
- *a hypnotized ghost that can't recall who he was in life,*
- *and Reggie his buffalito stuck in a saurian toilet...*

Can one man prevail against multiple alien races, a starship captain extortionist, and a planetary crime boss with a blood feud? To find out, you'll have to read the next novel, Buffalito Contingency.

Here's a taste:

"Don't pay it," said a new voice, one with too much gravel to belong to any Phloke I'd met thus far. I turned around but saw no one.

"Down here," said the voice.

I lowered my gaze and stared into a pair of protruding eyes set wide apart on a dusky green head. That head lacked hair, a nose or even nostrils, and its lipless mouth sported a pair of upward projecting tusks that gleamed like an advertisement for a phosphorus-based dentifrice. The head attached to the body in the usual way, resulting in a six-limbed biped that stood just over a meter in height. He looked for all the world like some midget version of a Thark, out of a twentieth century Burroughs's novel. Clearly I was hallucinating. Reggie stared at him, stuck out his tiny blue tongue as if to taste the air, and yipped.

"Don't accept any of those charges," said my figment. He lacked shirt and shoes, reminding me of those signs back on Earth that would have prevented him receiving any service. His only clothing was a pair of wheat-colored overalls made from a waxy upholstery fabric and riddled with at least a dozen pockets and pouches.

"Sir, you are interfering in a transaction that is none of your affair," said the manager, ribbons rustling.

"Baby it is, and baby it isn't," said the newcomer. "But I heard it all, and you're out of line charging him when you've violated the inter-alien comfort clause of the consortium of hostels, hotels, and sleep facilities, to which this resort is a signatory."

"I did no such thing."

"You put a human in a suite intended for a species twice his size. Did you also include any protective gear? Any supplemental aids? Any instructive guides? Hah! I can see the answer by the color of your ribbons. In fact, you didn't just fail to see to the comforts of this guest, but you're guilty of potentially endangering him as well!"

The manager's ribbons fluttered and tangled. "He's... he's not actually a guest, he's an employee of the resort."

"Don't get cute and technical," said the little green man. "The consortium doesn't care if he's your doorman's incontinent grandmother, if he sleeps under your roof, he's a guest. End of discussion. Perhaps you don't realize it, but Conroy is a famous human. He came to your resort expecting you would keep him safe from injury—"

"What injury? I see no injury!" The manager's tone had lost its velvety professionalism and acquired a distinct shrill.

"Are you a licensed physician? Do you feel competent to diagnose the first human being that's ever stayed in your facility? Don't worry, I'll take care of that, and I'll be sending you the appropriate reimbursement paperwork too. Before that though, I suggest you void the bill you were about to scam this guy into paying, and hope he doesn't pursue your flagrant breach of guest services and shut down your entire facility."

"I... I..."

"And send a repair crew up there to fix things. You can't expect the Amazing Conroy to wait around while you blow in the breeze. Stop wasting his time."

"I... yes, of course. I'm terribly sorry, Mr. Conroy. I'll see to it at once."

The little green alien reached up with both of its right hands and tugged on my arm. "C'mon, we've got things to discuss. Let's do it over breakfast. We can beat that whole post-dawn rush."

I pulled free and glanced back at the manager. He looked only too relieved to see us go. "What just happened here?"

"I saved you from a hotel scam and put the fear into them so they won't try that crap on you again."

"Who are you?"

He drew something from a pouch with a middle hand and shoved it at me, a rectangle of stiff, linen paper. I hadn't seen a business card since I'd left Earth. Printed on one side with gold ink were seven words:

IMPROBABLY MANAGEMENT:
A PLAN FOR EVERY CONTINGENCY.

I looked up from the card and into his protruding eyes.
"The name's Billi. I'm going to be your agent."

Continued in *Buffalito Contingency*

BONUS OFFER

THANKS FOR READING THIS BOOK

If you liked it, I hope you'll use the link below to join my Reader Group, where you'll receive my monthly newsletter with updates, special offers, contests, sneak peeks, and free fiction.

Just for signing up, I'll send you "Texas Fold'em," a solo story featuring Left-John Mocker, a professional gambler who is looking to recharge his luck.

https://bit.ly/LMS-join

ABOUT LAWRENCE M. SCHOEN

Lawrence M. Schoen holds a Ph.D. in cognitive psychology and psycholinguistics. He spent ten years as a college professor, teaching classes and doing research in the areas of human memory and language. This was followed by seventeen years as the director of research for a medical center in Philadelphia that provided mental health and addiction services.

He's also the founder of the Klingon Language Institute, and since 1992 has championed the exploration and use of this constructed tongue throughout the world. In addition, he works occasionally as a hypnotherapist specializing in authors' issues. And too, he is a cancer survivor.

In 2007, he was a finalist for the Astounding Award for Best New Writer. He received a Hugo Award nomination for Best Short Story in 2010 and Nebula Award nominations for Best Novella in

2013, 2014, 2015, and 2018, for Best Novelette in 2019, and for Best Novel in 2016.

Some of his most popular writing deals with the ongoing humorous adventures of a space-faring stage hypnotist named the Amazing Conroy and his companion animal, Reggie, an alien buffalito that can eat anything and farts oxygen. The universe he created for them has since spawned additional series involving galactic couriers and physics-defying pizza.

His *Barsk* series represents his more serious work and uses anthropomorphic SF to explore ideas of prophecy, intolerance, political betrayal, speaking to the dead, predestination, and free will. It's also earned him the Cóyotl Award for Best Novel of 2015, and again in 2018.

Lawrence lives near Philadelphia with his wife, Valerie, who is neither a psychologist nor a Klingon speaker.

f facebook.com/lawrencemschoen

🐦 twitter.com/klingonguy

a amazon.com/author/lawrenceschoen

g goodreads.com/lawrencemschoen

▶ youtube.com/Klingonguy

BB bookbub.com/authors/lawrence-m-schoen

ALSO BY LAWRENCE M. SCHOEN

Barsk

Barsk: The Elephants' Graveyard
(2015 Nebula Award Finalist, 2015 Winner Cóyotl Award)

The Moons of Barsk
(2018 Winner Cóyotl Award)

Excerpts of Jorl ben Tral

Soup of the Moment

Coming Soon!
Pizlo's Limits

SERIES IN THE "CONROYVERSE"

Conroyverse: A Sampler
("Buffalo Dogs," *Buffalito Destiny*, *Ace of Corpses*, and *Slice of Entropy*)

The Amazing Conroy

Buffalito Bundle
(includes "Yesterday's Taste," 2011 WSFA Small Press Award Finalist)

Barry's Tale
(2012 Nebula Award Finalist)

Calendrical Regression

(2014 Nebula Award Finalist)

Barry's Deal
(2017 Nebula Award Finalist)

Buffalito Destiny

Trial of the Century
(2013 Nebula Award Finalist)

Buffalito Contingency

Command Performance
(The Amazing Conroy Omnibus Edition)

Freelance Courier

Ace of Corpses

Ace of Saints

Ace of Thralls

Ace of Agency
(Freelance Courier Books 1 - 3)

Pizza In Space

Slice of Entropy

Coming Soon!
Slice of Chaos

Pirates of Sol

Pirates of Marz

Coming Soon!

Pirates of Erth

Seeds of War (with Jonathan Brazee)

Invasion

Scorched Earth

Bitter Harvest

Seeds of War Trilogy

Adrenaline Rush (with Brian Thorne)

Fight or Flight

Alien Thrill Seeker

Anger Management

Adrenaline Rush
(The Complete Series)

Coming Soon!

The Demon Codex Trilogy (with Brian Thorne)

Collections

Creature Academy:

Cautionary Poems of Public Education

Sweet Potato Pie and other stories

The Rule of Three and other stories

Openings without Closure

Non-Fiction

Eating Authors: One Hundred Writers'
Most Memorable Meals

Coming Soon!
Hypnosis for Writers

Author Website:

http://www.lawrencemschoen.com/books/